WHOSE CHICK ARE YOU?

NANCY TAFURI

Greenwillow Books

An Imprint of HarperCollinsPublishers

The sun was rising.

An egg was ready to hatch.

CHIRP!
CHIRP!

Whose egg is that?

And then ~

TAP!

PECK!

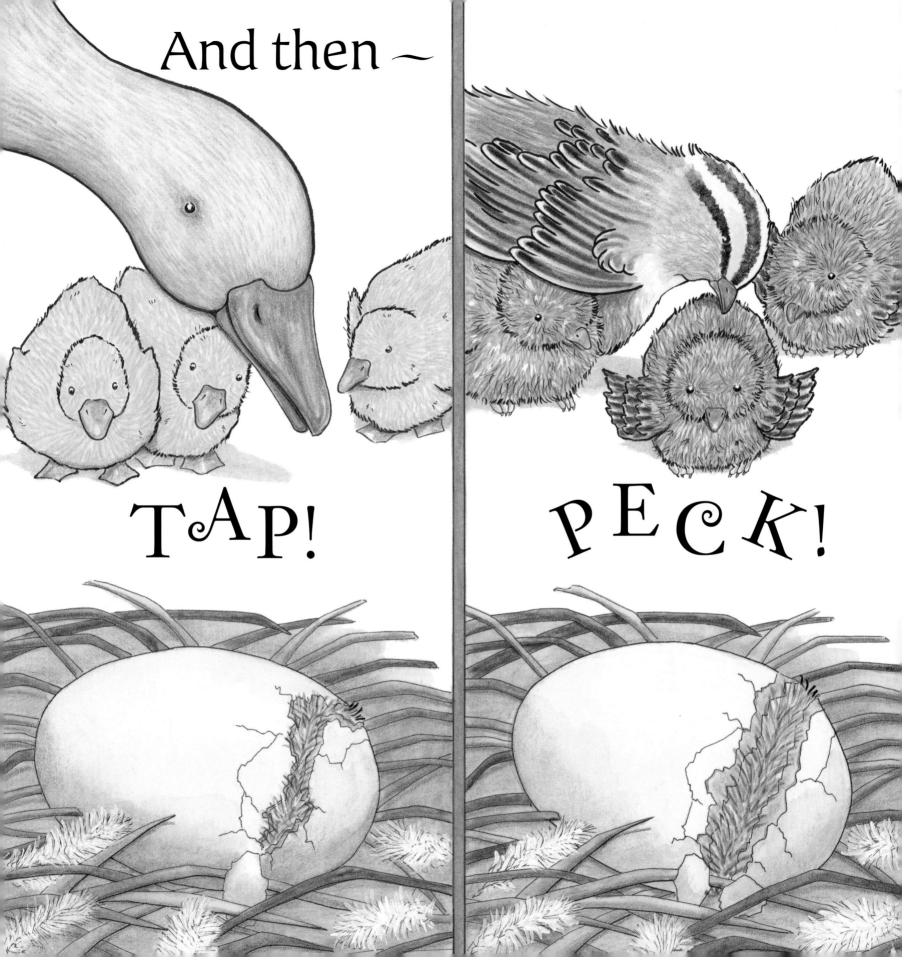

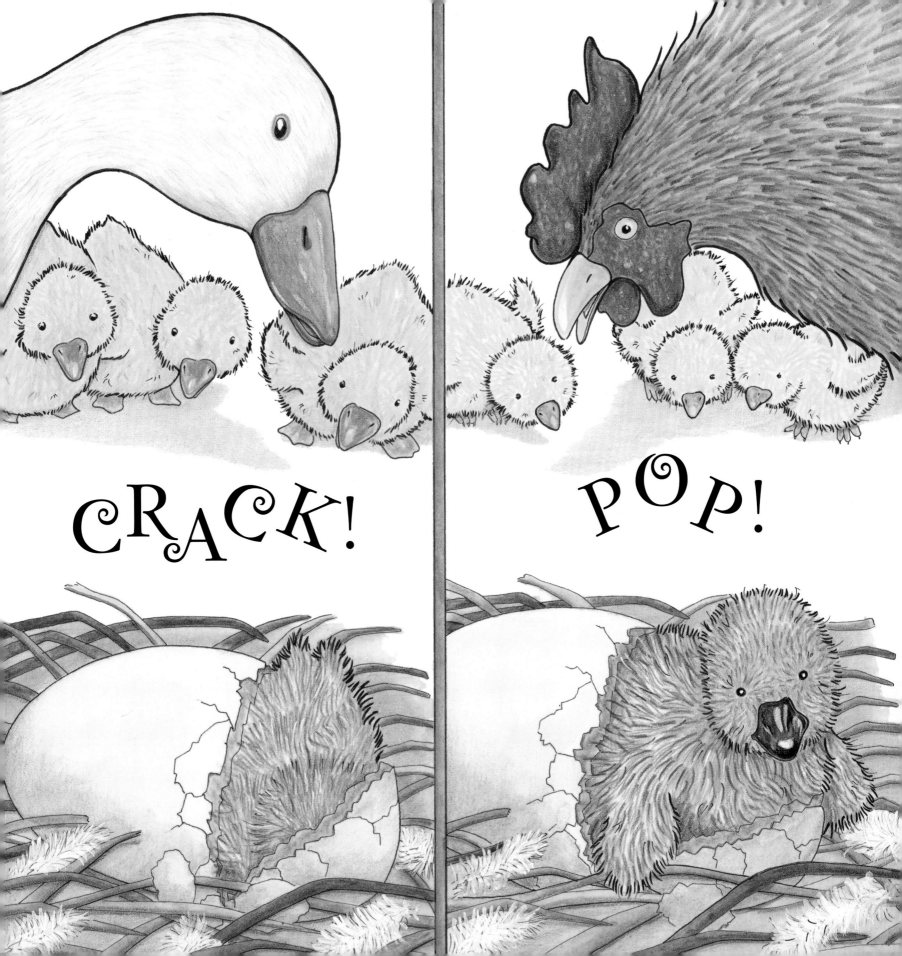

CRACK!

POP!

CLUCK! QUACK! CHIRP! HONK!

Whose chick are you?

Goose didn't know.
Duck didn't know.

Hen didn't know.
Bird didn't know.

And Little Chick
didn't know.

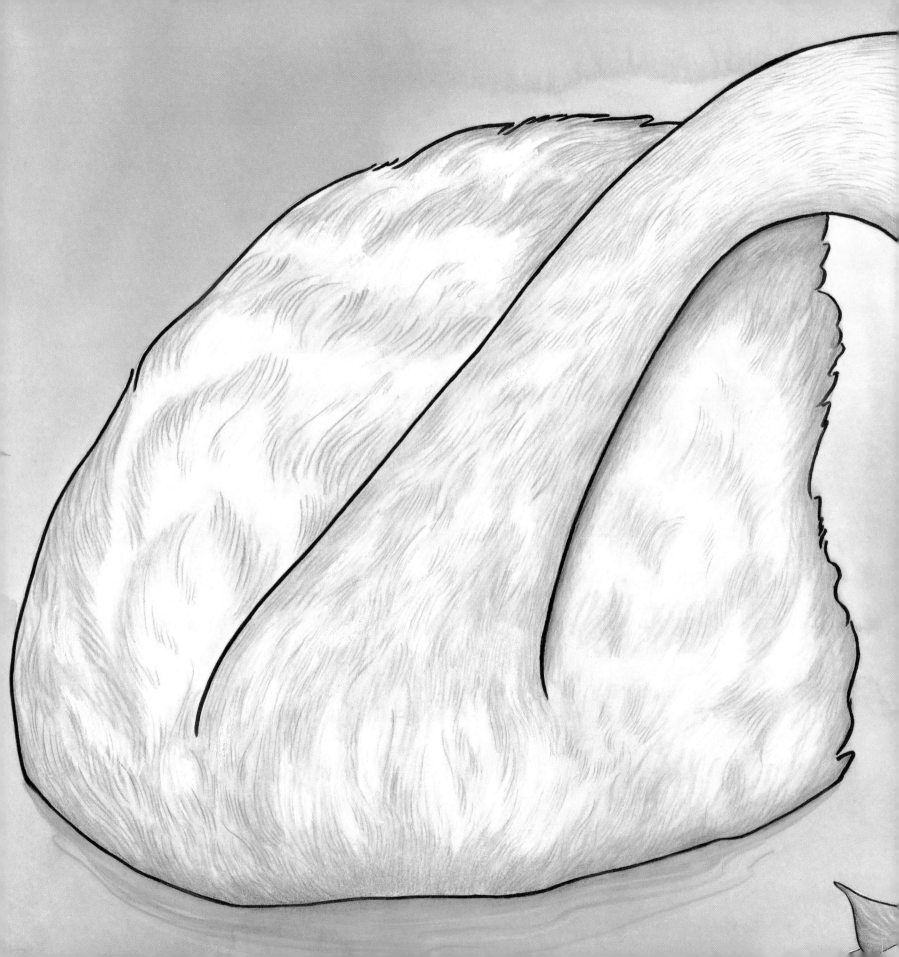

But Swan
knew whose chick
this was ~

it was hers!

And Little Chick
was very happy!
CROO!
CROO!

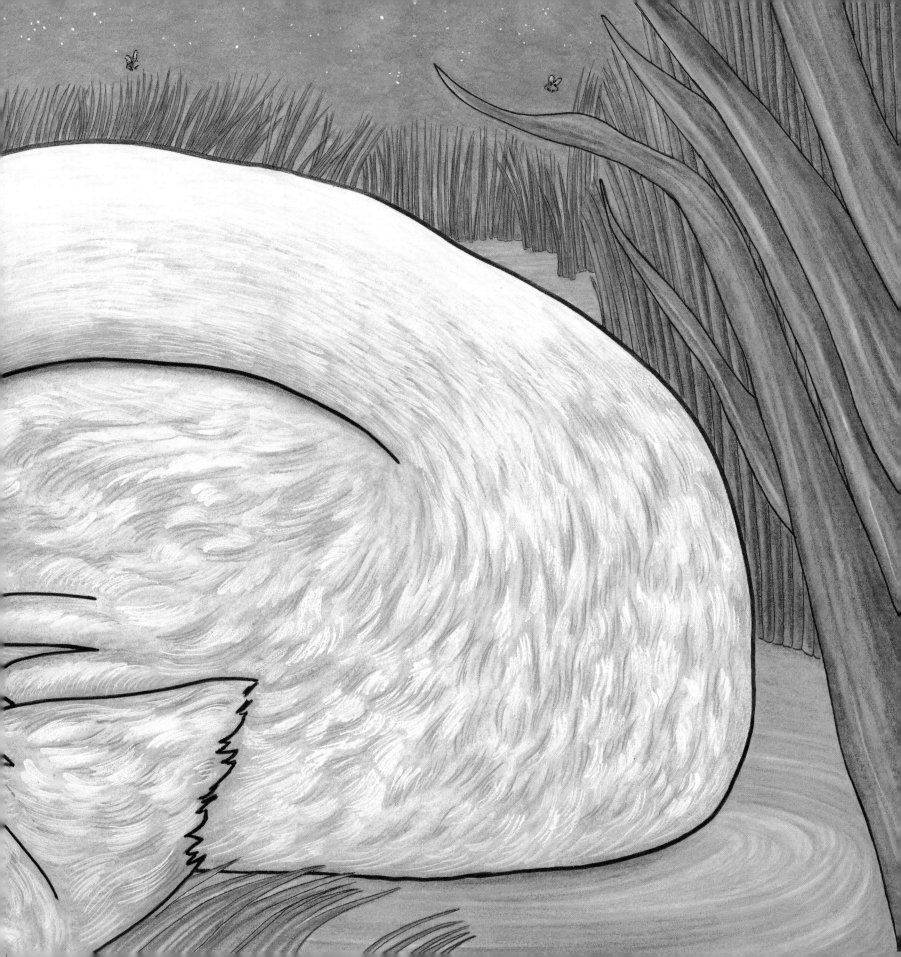

For my little chick

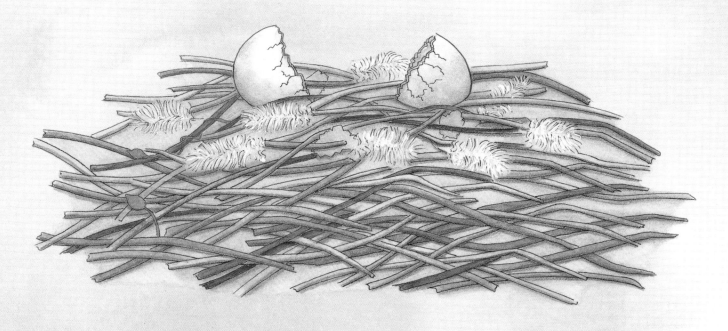

Whose Chick Are You?
Copyright © 2007 by Nancy Tafuri
All rights reserved. Manufactured in China.
www.harpercollinschildrens.com

Brush pen and watercolor paints were used to prepare the full-color art.
The text type is Laricio.

Library of Congress Cataloging-in-Publication Data
Whose chick are you? / by Nancy Tafuri.
p. cm.
"Greenwillow Books."
Summary: Goose, Duck, Hen, Bird, and the little chick itself
cannot tell to whom a new hatchling belongs, but its mother knows.
ISBN-10: 0-06-082514-6 (trade bdg.) ISBN-13: 978-0-06-082514-0 (trade bdg.)
ISBN-10: 0-06-082515-4 (lib. bdg.) ISBN-13: 978-0-06-082515-7 (lib. bdg.)
[1. Mother and child—Fiction. 2. Eggs—Fiction. 3. Swans—Fiction. 4. Birds—Fiction.] I. Title.
PZ7.T117Who 2005 [E]—dc22 2005046020

First Edition 10 9 8 7 6 5 4 3 2 1

Greenwillow Books